Special thank you to
The Writer's Workshop of Bloomingdale

All rights reserved. No part of this publication may be reproduced in whole or in part, or stored in a retrieval system, or transmitted in any form or by any means, electronics, mechanical, photocopying, recording, or otherwise, without written permission from the author and artist. For information regarding permission, send email to rina.yoeu@mail.com.

ISBN 9781468067163

Text copyright © 2012 by Rina S. Yoeu.
Illustrations copyright © 2012 by Emily A. Rohman.

For Farid

Thiago and the Beast

Once there was a boy named Thiago. He was always the first to the storyteller's circle. He could not wait to hear more about the mysterious events on the other side of the river. But tonight, the storyteller began with a warning.

"I can see the curiosity in your eyes, Thiago, but you must never cross the river," the storyteller began. "A monster lives there. And it will eat you."

The village elder added, "And it storms at night. The thunder roars until the earth trembles."

"The waves are too strong, son," his father said.

"You won't make it to the other side of the shore."

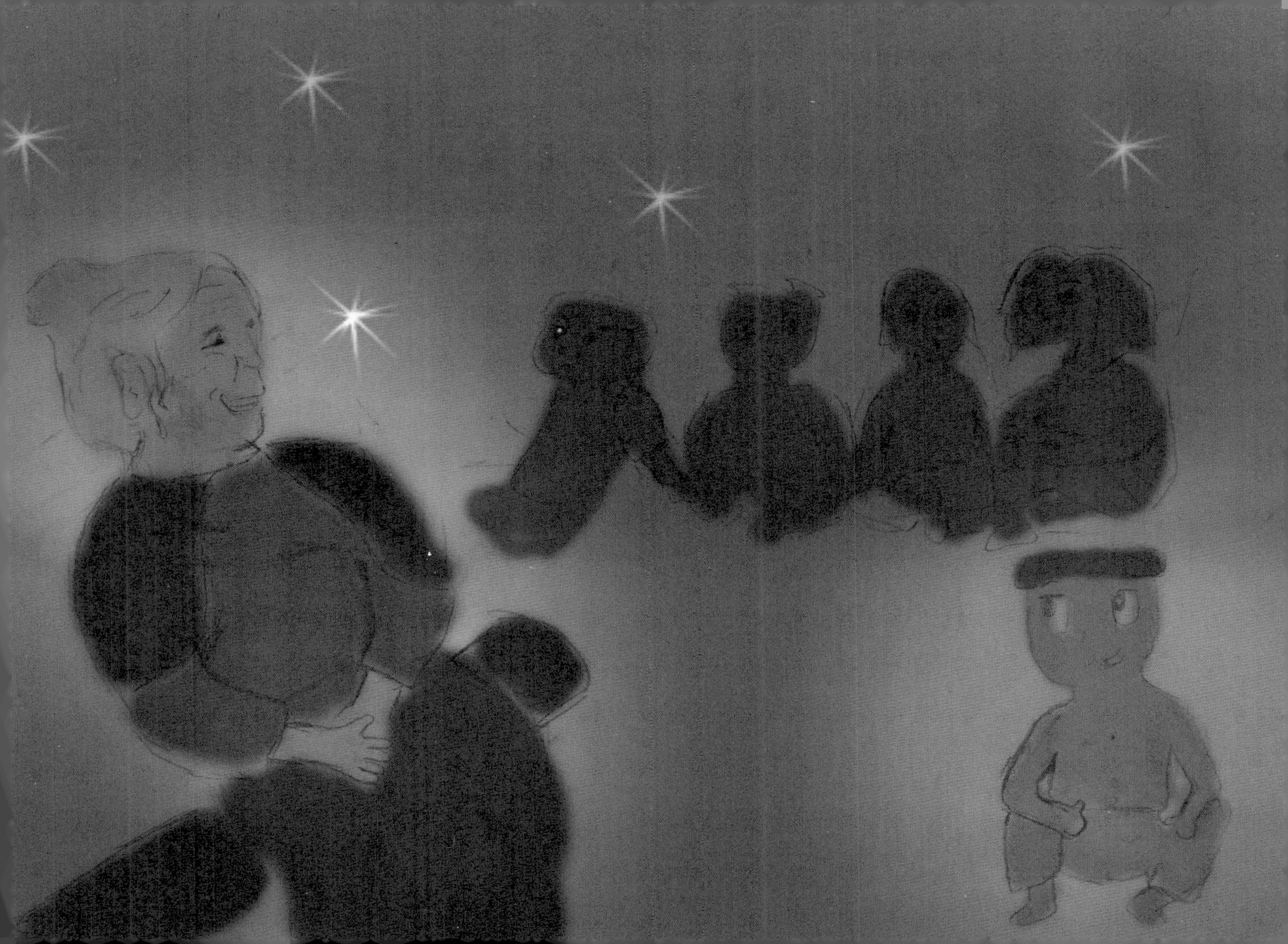

When the sun peeked through the horizon, Thiago ventured off to the river. He tossed a fishing spear and a basket into the boat. He untied the boat from a snag and headed away from the bank looking for fish. He waited and waited, but not a fish swam by. He paddled toward the middle of the river; still no fish.

"I must catch fish," he said.

Thiago rowed in circles and wondered where all the fish were. He glanced toward his village. Then, he looked toward the other side of the river, the place everyone told him not to go. The thought of going there gave him goose bumps. But he did it anyway.

When he was on the other side of the river, Thiago could not believe his eyes.
"So many fish!" he screamed.

He plopped down on the edge of the boat and plunged his hand into the water. He felt a fish bump in his palm. He stood up and grabbed his fishing stick. He speared one fish and another. And another until the basket overflowed with fish.

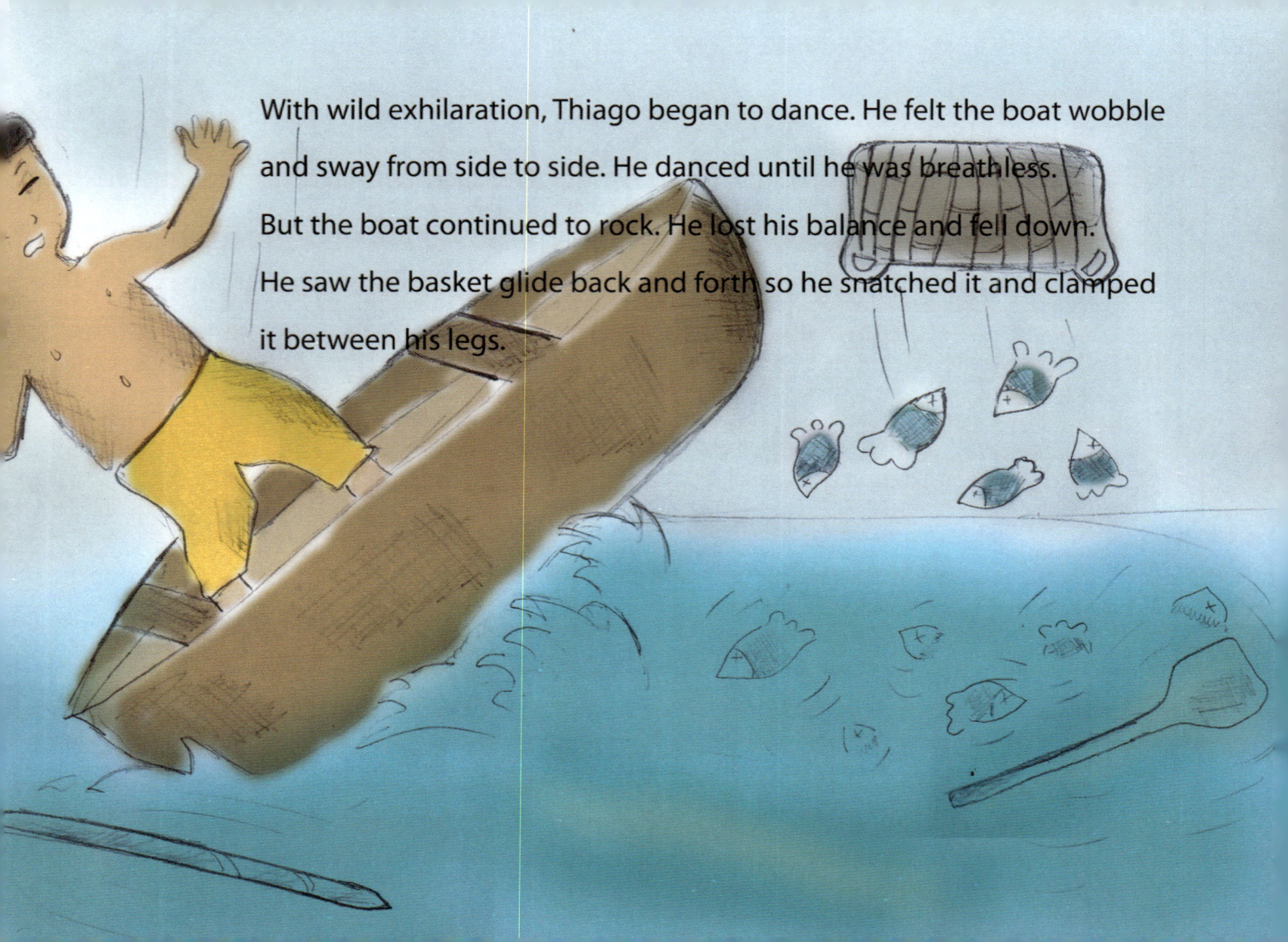

With wild exhilaration, Thiago began to dance. He felt the boat wobble and sway from side to side. He danced until he was breathless. But the boat continued to rock. He lost his balance and fell down. He saw the basket glide back and forth so he snatched it and clamped it between his legs.

The river kicked up a wave and tipped the boat to one side. He gasped as he watched the basket fly into the air. Then, it came back down, dumping the fish right back into the river.

He held on tight to the side of the boat as it was tossed about by the river's tantrum.

Another violent wave slapped Thiago in the face and knocked him off the boat. He could see that he was sinking to the bottom. As soon as his feet touched the river's floor, he pushed himself up to the surface, coughing up water.

Thiago swam to the forbidden shore.

Thiago forced himself off the ground. With great pain, he dragged his feet into the forest. As he shuffled along, he saw a tree laden with red fruit and rats scurry across the roots of the trees. Sore from the boat incident, he lowered his achy body and leaned against the foot of a tree. How would he ever get home?

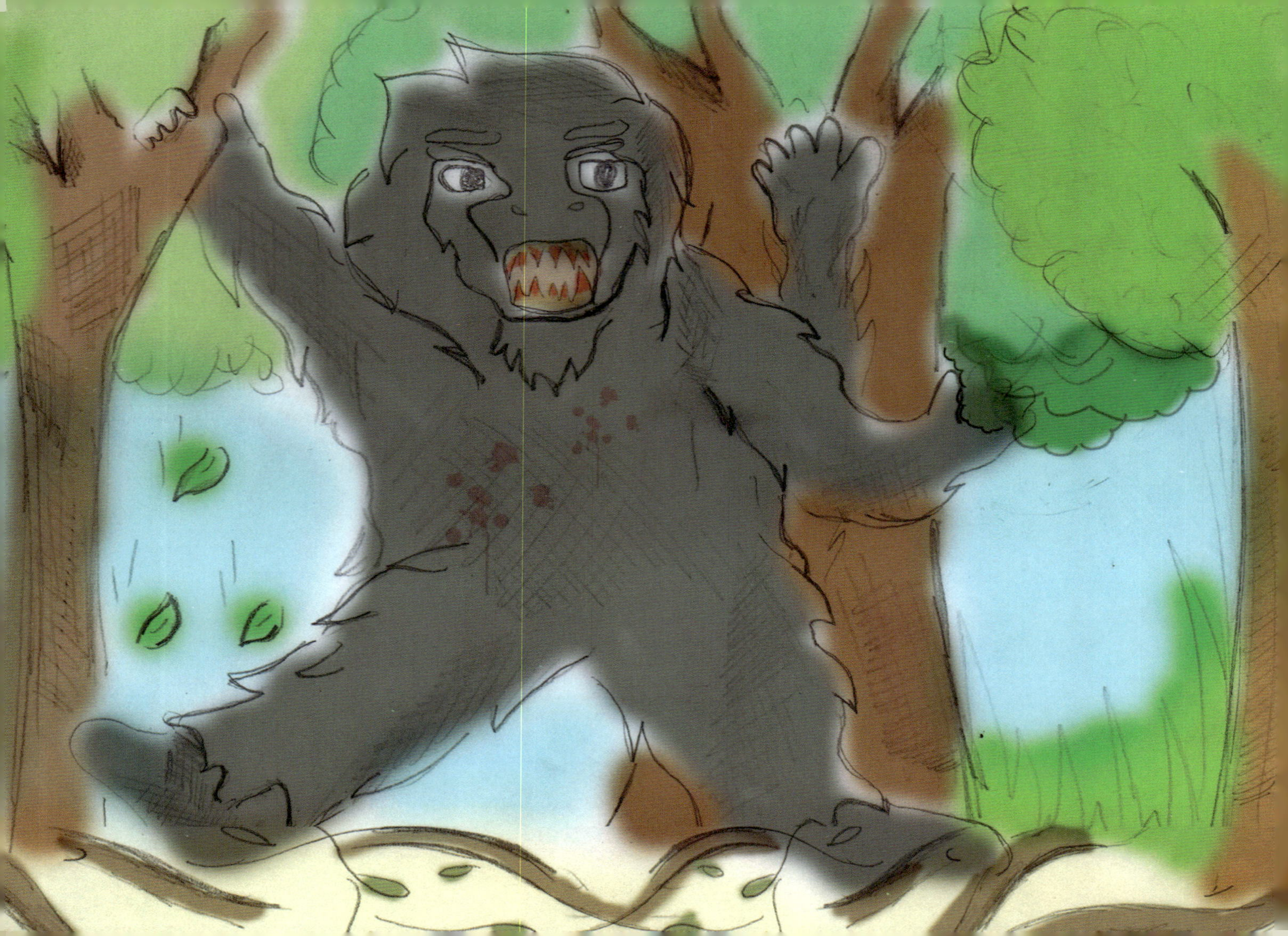

A rumbling sound coming from a bush startled Thiago. He stood up, listening for the noise. The bush rattled. Then he heard *urr! urr!*

"Who's...who's...who's there?" Thiago stammered.

The bush parted. A black woolly animal emerged. Thiago tilted his head to stare at the beast's large eyes, flared nostrils, and jagged red teeth.

When the beast stomped the ground, the trees shook and the rats dashed into their burrows.

Thiago ran away from the beast. He tripped on a log and fell. The ground beneath him caved in. He tumbled down into a cave filled with rats. He felt them scamper all over his body, crawl underneath his legs, and claw at his dark hair. Horrified, Thiago sprang up. "Help me! Help me!" he screamed.

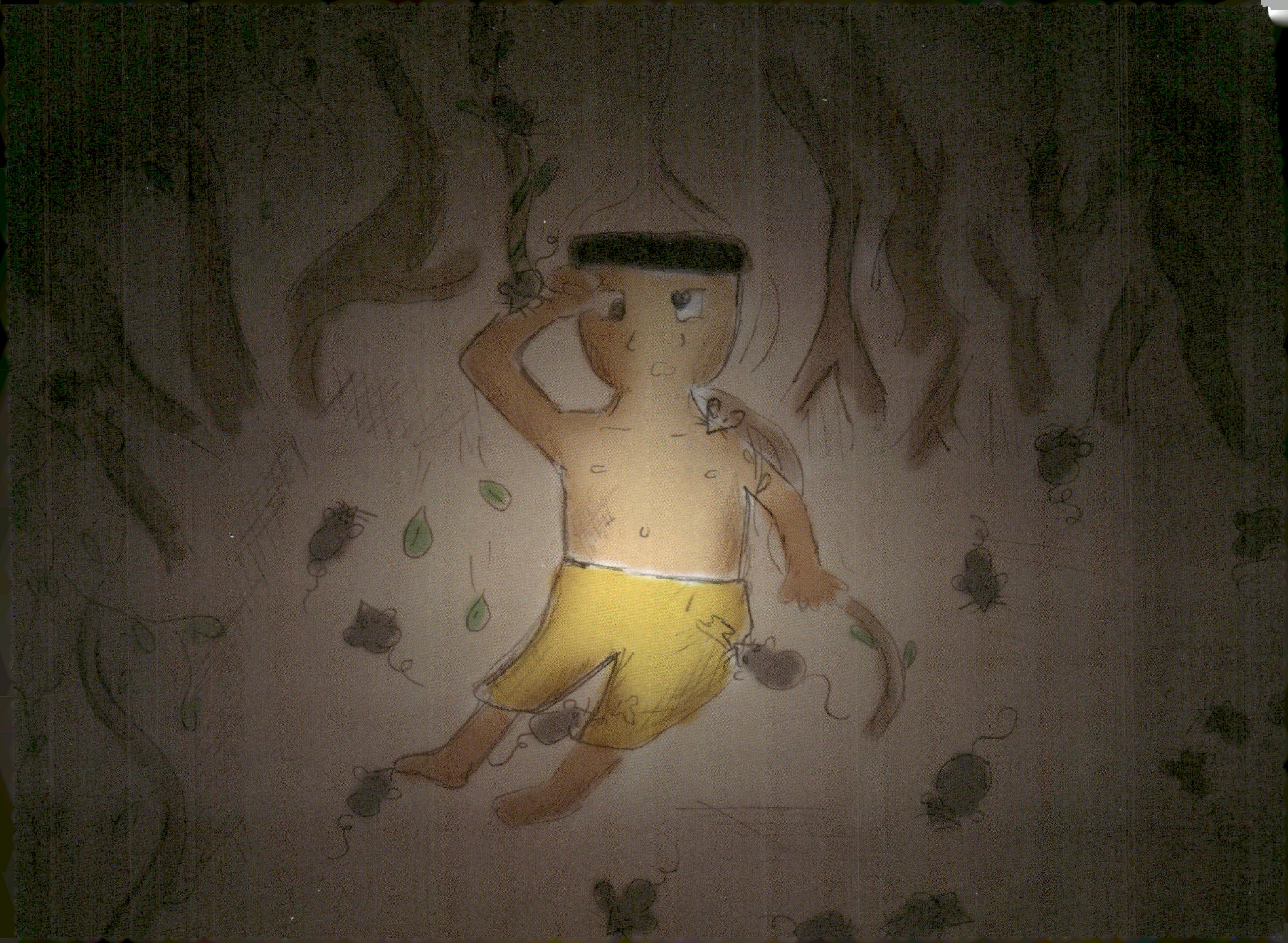

Thiago looked down at his feet and felt the rats clawing his skin. Then, he looked up and saw the beast offering a hand to him. He wanted to get out of the rat-infested hole, so he tried to reach for the hand, but it was too far. He jumped and jumped and jumped. But still he could not reach it. The beast got up and backed away from the deep hole.

"Don't leave me in here, please!" Thiago begged.

Thiago cringed at the rats circling his feet. He began to climb. He placed one foot on a twisted root. He grabbed onto a vine above and placed his other foot on another root. As he climbed, he felt a rat scuttle down his arm and bit his finger. "Ahh!"

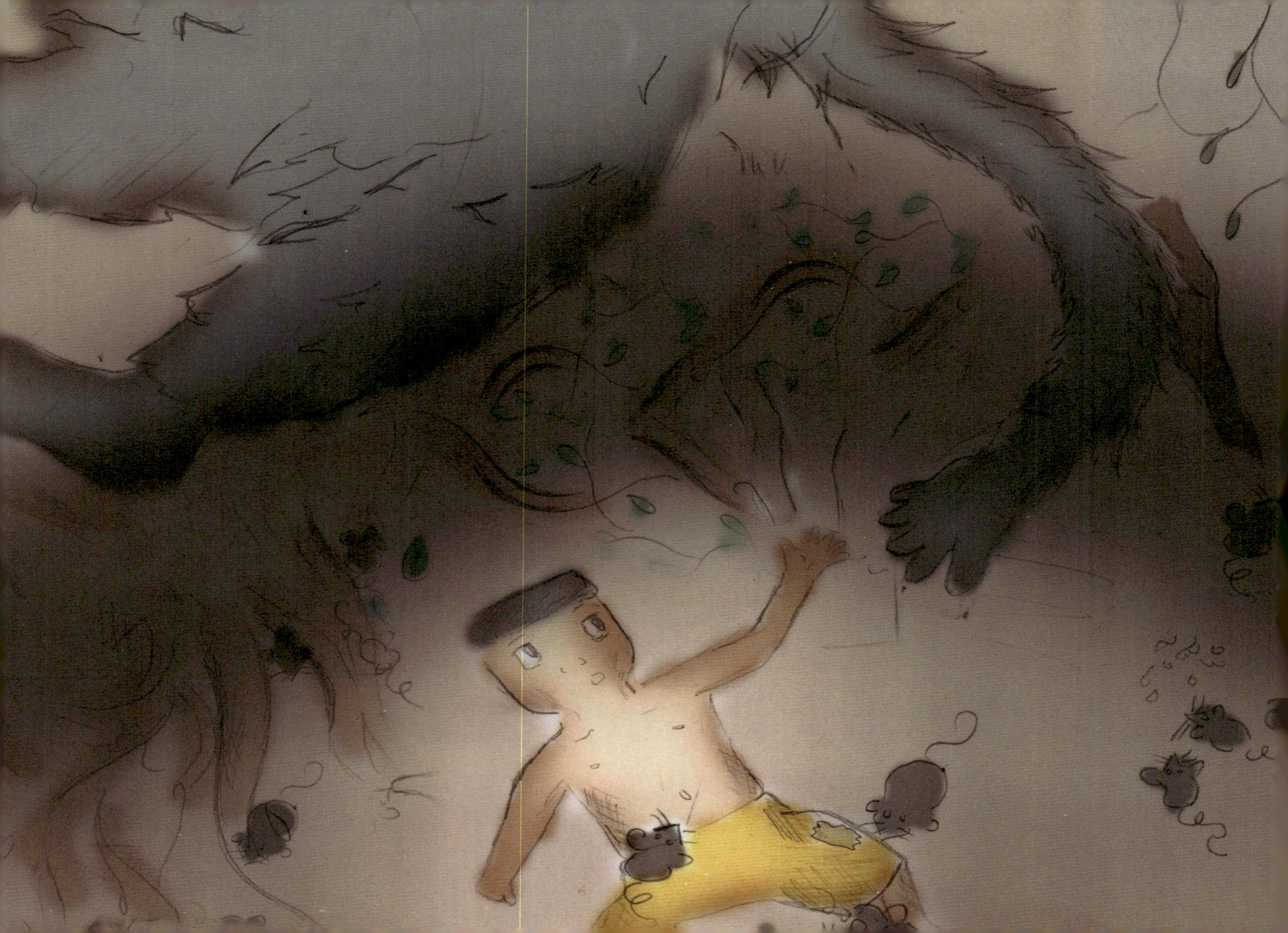

He lost his footing and tumbled back into the cave. Splaying on the ground, Thiago looked up and saw the beast standing backward at the edge of the pit. It had a thick vine loop around the waist, and its unusual tail was reaching down to him.

Thiago stood up staring at the tail. "Ahh," Thiago said. "A tail-hand."

He grabbed the tail-hand. He felt the velvety grip of the tail-hand as his body rose from the cave.

"Thanks, Beast. May I call you Beast?"

Beast nodded.

The forest began to grow darker.

Thiago was not fearful now sitting under the towering tree next to Beast. When it was pitch-black, Thiago saw bright lights twinkling against the sky. More lights appeared, spotlighting the forest. Then, the roots of the trees glowed fluorescent green; the ones behind him projected yellow, and in the middle of the forest emerged red and blue and purple lights.

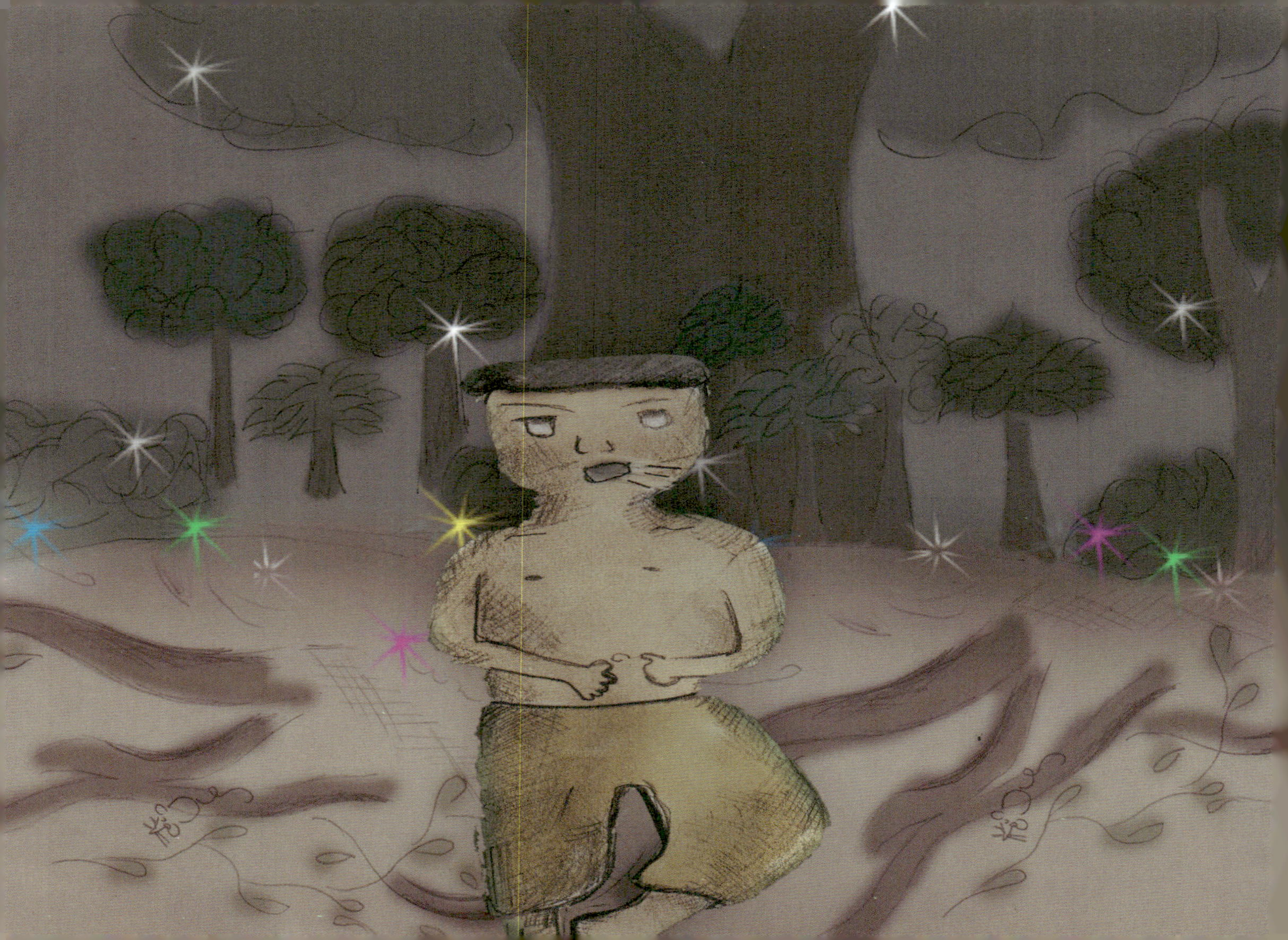

Thiago stood up, flabbergasted. While he was watching the colorful lights, the sounds from the branches rattling and the red fruit drumming down to the ground roared through the air like a stormy night. He tilted his head to the sky and smiled, remembering the village elder's tale. At this moment he knew that the village elder's story was nothing like she had said, it was just the opposite.

The next morning, Thiago and Beast gathered logs, branches, and vines. Then they dragged them to the shore.

Standing knee deep in the river, they assembled a raft. Thiago looked across the river and pointed, "That's my home."

"Urr," Beast acknowledged.

"I'll come and visit you," Thiago said.

"Urr! Urr!" Beast roared.

Thiago waved good-bye as he headed home.

He could not wait to tell everyone about Beast.